W9-BHB-136

Dear Molly,
Dear Olive

Molly Meets Trouble
(Whose Real Name Is Jenna)

written by
Megan Atwood

illustrated by
Lucy Fleming

Capstone Young Readers
a capstone imprint

225900

Dear Molly, Dear Olive is published by Capstone Young Readers,
a Capstone Imprint
1710 Roe Crest Drive
North Mankato, Minnesota 56003
www.mycapstone.com

Copyright © 2017 Capstone Young Readers

All rights reserved. No part of this publication may be reproduced in whole or in part,
or stored in a retrieval system, or transmitted in any form or by any means, electronic,
mechanical, photocopying, recording,
or otherwise, without written permission of the publisher.

Library of Congress Cataloging-in-Publication Data
Names: Atwood, Megan, author. | Fleming, Lucy, illustrator.
Title: Molly meets trouble (whose real name is Jenna) /
by Megan Atwood; [illustrated by Lucy Fleming].
Description: North Mankato, Minnesota: Picture Window Books, an imprint of Capstone
Press, [2017] | Series: Dear Molly, Dear Olive | Summary: Pen pals Molly and Olive are
both having relationship problems in their fourth grade classes—Molly is struggling with
Jenna, a new girl, who seems to think that name-calling is a way to fit in, and Olive has
joined a gymnastics team, which is putting a strain on her friendship with Emma, whom
she has known for years.
Identifiers: LCCN 2016010940 | ISBN 9781479586967 (library binding) |
ISBN 9781623706180 (paperback) | ISBN 9781479587001 (ebook (pdf))
Subjects: LCSH: Best friends—Juvenile fiction. | Friendship—Juvenile fiction. | Pen
pals—Juvenile fiction. | Letter writing—Juvenile fiction. | Interpersonal relations—
Juvenile fiction. | Elementary schools—Juvenile fiction. | New York (N.Y.)—Juvenile
fiction. | Iowa—Juvenile fiction. | CYAC: Best friends—Fiction. | Friendship—Fiction.
| Pen pals—Fiction. | Letter writing—Fiction. | Interpersonal relations—Fiction. |
Schools—Fiction. | New York (N.Y.)—Fiction. | Iowa—Fiction.
Classification: LCC PZ7.A8952 Mq 2017 | DDC 813.6—dc23
LC record available at http://lccn.loc.gov/2016010940

Designers: Aruna Rangarajan and Tracy McCabe

Design Elements: Shutterstock

Printed in Canada.
032016   009642F16

Table of Contents

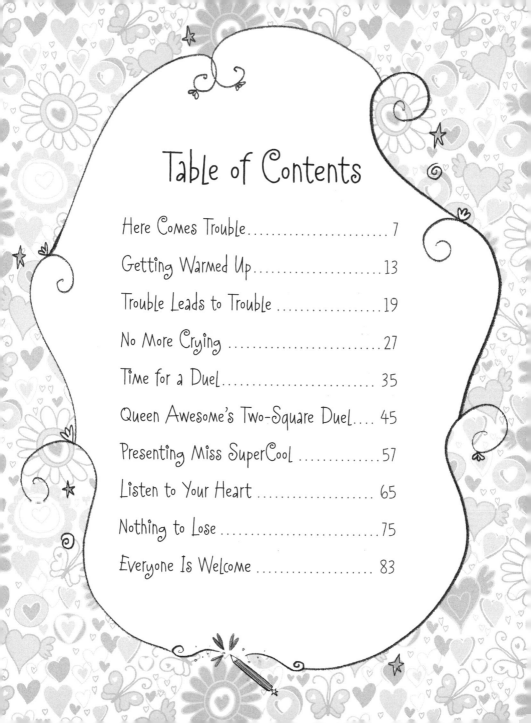

Dear Molly,
Dear Olive

Molly and Olive are best friends — best friends who've never met! Two years ago, in second grade, they signed up for a cross-country Pen Pal Club. Their friendship was instant.

Molly and Olive send each other letters and email. They send postcards, notes, and little gifts too. Molly lives in New York City with her mom and younger brother. Olive lives on a farm near Sergeant Bluff, Iowa, with her parents. The girls' lives are very different from one another. But Molly and Olive understand each other better than anyone.

6

Chapter 1

Here Comes Trouble

Molly

Dear Olive,

Surprise! Cool necklace, huh? My mom got it on her way to the subway. She thought of us right away. There are two halves. I'm wearing the other half. Mine says FRIENDS. Yours says BEST. Get it? We're BEST FRIENDS. We'll always be together when we wear our friendship necklaces.

We're still best friends, right? A new girl at school told everyone that I don't have any friends. I told her about you, but she said I made you up. My IMAGINARY friend. Ha! Could an imaginary friend wear a necklace? No. It would fall right to the ground. Duh.

Gotta run. I'm playing a new trick on Damien. I'm going to tell him that Mom is an alien in disguise. The only way to see her true form is to throw water on her. Should be a fun dinner!

Your best REAL friend,

Molly

SEND MORE MAIL

The day I met Trouble (whose real name is Jenna) was NOT a good day. It all started at recess, when she called me a boogerhead . . .

"Am not!" I yelled.

"Are too!" Jenna yelled back.

I stamped my foot. "Am not!"

"Are too!"

Things were not going well.

No one was going to win this shouting match. So I scooped up an armful of leaves and threw them at Jenna's head. Sometimes that's what you have to do: You have to throw leaves.

But NOT when your teacher, Ms. Harter, is standing right there. Oops!

"Molly! We don't throw leaves at each other," Ms. Harter said.

That wasn't true, because I HAD just thrown leaves. I was going to say that, but Jenna spoke first. She made her eyes real big.

"Ms. Harter," Jenna said, "I didn't do anything. Really! I was just standing here."

I opened my mouth, but no words came out. She *didn't do*

anything? Ha! She started it! This wasn't fair. So I did the only thing I could. I scooped up more leaves and threw them at her head again. Now she looked like a tree. A big lying tree. A Liar Tree.

Sometimes, like I said, you just have to throw leaves.

Ms. Harter shook her head. "Molly, go to the principal's office," she said. "Now."

"Fine," I said, "but she's a Liar Tree."

Jenna stuck out her tongue at me, then pulled it back in real fast. Ms. Harter didn't see. I stomped away.

I WANTED to go to the principal's office. Principal Martinez knew me pretty well. She and my mom had grown up together. I was sure she'd be on my side. Jenna hadn't been at my school more than a week. But right away she started being mean to me. Maybe Principal Martinez could tell me why.

Chapter 2

Getting Warmed Up

Olive

Dear Molly,

My mom says I should write "dear" when I write a paper letter to someone. I wanted to write you a paper letter instead of an email. I got the necklace, and I LOVE IT. It's my favorite necklace ever.

We will always be best friends. Always. Show the new girl a picture of me. Then she'll know I'm real!

I just tried out for the Sioux City gymnastics team. I made it! My first practice is tomorrow. A lot of the girls go to my school, but I don't know them very well. They have been on the team for a couple years already. I really hope they like me. It would be nice to make new friends here. I love gymnastics SO MUCH. This is a dream come true.

Thank you for the necklace! I'll send you something real soon.

ALWAYS your best friend,

Olive

P.S. Did Damien throw water on your mom? Did he get in trouble? Sometimes I wish I had a little brother or sister.

WRITE SOON

When my mom and I walked in, I heard all the sounds I was used to from my little gym. I heard the *THUMP, THUMP, THUMP* of feet hitting the floor. I heard the *THWACK* of the springboard. Only it sounded like there were one thousand more thumps and thwacks here. Coach Stanley saw me and came over.

"Hey, Olive," he said. "Are you ready for your first practice in the big city? This is a little different from Sergeant Bluff, isn't it?"

I didn't know what to say. I nodded. Sioux City was HUGE. It was only fifteen miles from my hometown, but it was one million times bigger. So was this gym.

A couple of girls I recognized from tryouts stood in the back of the gym. They stood together in line for the balance beam and whispered. I relaxed a little. The balance beam was my favorite. I just learned how to do a back handspring on it. I couldn't quite stick the landing, though. Not yet.

I saw the next girl in line get on the balance beam. She did a perfect back handspring.

"The girls are just warming up," Coach said. "You can throw your bag over there and then join the team."

I looked up at Mom. "I don't think I can do this," I whispered.

She squeezed me super tight. I loved my mom's squeezes. Right then I wished she would squeeze me all the way home.

"Olive, you've always wanted to do this," she said. "New things can be scary. But I promise you, it will work out." She took my bag off my shoulder. "Now give me your sweats, and go get 'em. I'll be sitting over there."

I still wasn't sure this was a good idea. But I did what my mom said.

The girls looked at me and then looked away. No one said hi or anything. I felt like I had horns on my head! I tried to just keep my head down and practice.

But when practice started, I messed up almost every move. Everyone probably wondered why I was even on the team.

On the way home, I had tears in my eyes, but I didn't let my mom see. I really wished Molly could have been there.

 Chapter 3

Trouble Leads to Trouble

"Molly," Principal Martinez said, "I love to see you. But not in here. What's going on?"

I was still mad. It was all Liar Tree's fault. But I didn't want to get her in trouble either. Snitching is for babies. So I decided to talk in code. I was sure Principal Martinez would understand me.

"Principal Martinez," I started, "I know a girl. I know her really well. Her name is . . ." I thought fast. I didn't want Principal Martinez to know the story was about me and Jenna.

"Her name is DOLLY. And there's another girl named . . . LIAR."

Principal Martinez leaned back in her chair. She had a funny smile on her face.

"Liar just came to this school," I continued. "She's being mean to Dolly. And I don't know why! She's spreading lies about me — I mean, about DOLLY."

I could feel the tears coming.

Principal Martinez nodded. "Yes, that's not very nice at all," she said. "Has Dolly tried to talk to . . . Liar?"

"No!" I said. "We haven't even — I mean, THEY haven't even talked. So why would she say bad things about me? I mean, HER. DOLLY, that is."

Principal Martinez got up and walked around the desk. "Molly, this sounds like the start of some bullying," she said. "You know, bullying is never okay. I think your friend Dolly should come talk to me. Then we can talk to her mom."

I slumped down in my seat. I didn't want to tell my mom. She'd think I was being a baby.

"Oh, never mind," I said. "Dolly is probably just making up things. Ha, ha."

Principal Martinez nodded. "Well, we should take Dolly seriously," she said. "But until she's ready to talk to me, maybe Dolly could talk to Liar — if she feels safe. Maybe Liar is scared. She's new in school. Sometimes people do strange things when they're scared."

I didn't think Jenna was frightened at all. And maybe that was the problem. That's when I got my idea. I could make Jenna scared to mess with me. She was saying bad things about ME, so I would say bad things about HER. I sat up and smiled big.

"Thanks, Principal Martinez!" I said, heading toward the door.

"Wait, wait, wait," she said. "You didn't tell me why you were sent to my office."

"Oh," I said, "I threw leaves at a girl's head."

"Well, then," Principal Martinez said. "Next recess, Molly, you'll be on raking duty."

Ugh.

Raking duty is the worst. How can trees have so many leaves? Seriously! I put on a good show, though. I groaned and held my back. I hoped Mr. Johnson, the groundskeeper, would let me go early. But he just kept humming and whistling.

Six big bags later, I was done. There was still some time for recess, so I ran over to my friends. They were playing four square. I love four square! I'm real good at it too. I stood in line and kept an eye on Jenna. She was sitting on the swings by herself. Time for my plan.

I tapped the girl in front of me on the shoulder. It was Lacey Anderson. She loved to gossip. Perfect.

"Hey," I said, "did you know the new girl has head lice?" I had to stop myself from giggling.

"Ew!" Lacey said.

I made my eyes real wide and said, "I know, right? I saw her scratching her head in gym class. So gross."

Then Lacey turned to the person in front of her and whispered. Soon everyone in line was whispering and looking at Jenna. A couple boys pointed. They scratched their heads, made weird noises, and laughed. My plan worked. And it wasn't hard at all.

Jenna didn't say anything. She looked down at the ground and then looked away.

I should have felt great. After all she had made up lies about me and my "imaginary

friend." But I felt bad for her. I felt so bad that my eyes got kind of watery. I couldn't tell Olive what I'd done. She might not want to be my best friend anymore.

The bell rang, and we all went back to class. My stomach hurt the rest of the day.

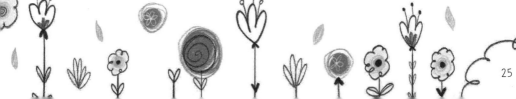

Chapter 4

No More Crying

Olive

I cried myself to sleep after the first gymnastics practice. Not fun! But I made a decision: NO. MORE. CRYING. I would just have to get better at gymnastics. Then the girls would talk to me. They probably thought I was bad for the team. I would show them I was a good team member.

I started going to my school gym with Mom early in the mornings to practice. The first morning I did one back handspring after another on the balance beam. I fell off A LOT. But just before Mom was about to leave, I stuck the landing. I STUCK the landing! I did a little happy dance and yelled.

That's when I saw a ponytail out of the corner of my eye. It looked like one of my teammates, Erika. I couldn't wait to tell her about my back handspring.

At lunch time I normally sat with my friend Emma. But she had made some new friends at Earth Club and sat with them now. I looked around the lunchroom for my teammates.

There they were. Erika, Haley, Ruth, and Elsa all sat together at a table. I had never noticed them before because I sat with Emma all the time. The four girls hunched over their trays and talked.

I took a deep breath and walked toward them. When I got a table away, they all stopped talking and stared at me. They weren't smiling. I didn't know what to do. Emma and her new friends waved at me.

"Olive!" Emma yelled. "Over here!" I turned and walked away from my teammates' table.

 So far, being on the city gymnastics team was not that great.

That night I got an email from Molly.

Dear Olive,

You won't believe it! You remember that new girl,

Jenna? I call her Liar Tree. First she got me sent to the principal's office. Then she spread lies about me all over school. She told Max, who told Lacey, who told Trevor, who told the whole fourth grade that I like eating boogers. GROSS! You know what else? She told everyone that I spit in people's lunches. So now no one wants to be around me at lunch. I need a way to get back at her. Any ideas?

Your best friend,

Molly

P.S. How was your first practice?

When I got the email, I got so mad for Molly. Only mean people say bad things about other people. Just like only mean people don't smile at their new teammate at lunch.

I wrote back to Molly right away.

Molly, I'm so sorry! That Jenna girl seems mean.
I think people who make things up are not very nice.
Maybe you should tell your teacher. Or your mom.
They might be able to help. Getting back at her will
just get you in more trouble. You already got sent to
the principal's office, right?

I chewed on my lip. I thought about telling
Molly about gymnastics. But I couldn't do it.
I couldn't tell her how bad I was. I couldn't tell
her how the girls wouldn't talk to me. Besides
I'd been to only one practice so far. I ended the
email fast.

I am squeezing my necklace right
now. Can you feel it? It means you're
getting a hug from me. Let me
know what happens with the

mean girl. You shouldn't have to deal with someone like that.

Your best friend,

Olive

I went to sleep feeling okay. Tomorrow was my second after-school practice. I'd show Erika, Ruth, Haley, and Elsa that I could do a perfect back handspring. They would see that I deserved to be on the team. Maybe then they'd like me.

Mom and I got into Sioux City early. I ran into the locker room and put on my shirt and shorts. None of the other girls were there yet. I did some stretches to warm up.

Once everyone arrived it was time for drills. Erika stood behind me in line. I took a big, deep breath and turned around. I was going to be brave and talk to her. But she wasn't looking at me.

When it was my turn on the beam, I did a back handspring. Even better? I did TWO back handsprings in a row AND stuck the landing! That was the first time I had EVER done that. Coach Stanley was so excited he thumped his clipboard. Erika and the rest of the team HAD to like me now. I'd proven I belonged here.

But the look on their faces was not happy.

So much for my plan.

Time for a Duel

After I got the email from Olive, I felt terrible. She said people who say bad things about other people aren't nice. I had said some bad things about Jenna.

After I told everyone that Jenna had head lice, Jenna said I ate boogers. I told everyone that Jenna had Smell-o-stinkitis. Then Jenna told everyone I spit in people's lunches. That wasn't true at all. I'd only pretended to do that once. Last year. In third grade. Jenna wasn't even there!

I didn't know what to do. If I told my mom, I'd have to tell her EVERYTHING. And everything included a bunch of lies. Ugh.

I didn't even feel like teasing Damien at dinner. In fact I felt so bad, I actually talked to him. That was my first mistake.

"Damien, how was your day?" I asked. I passed him some bread and smiled wide.

Mom looked at me like I'd grown a second head. She squinted. I knew that look. It was her "What are you up to?" look. It's not a good look. Really. Trust me.

"Nothing!" I shouted.

I slapped my hands over my mouth. Second mistake. Mom hadn't asked me anything! That was a sure sign I was doing something wrong.

"Molly Riley," Mom said.

"Nothing!" I said again. I kicked Damien hard under the table. "I SAID, how was your day, dummy!"

"Ow!" he squealed.

"Molly," Mom said, frowning, "you know how this works. If you tell me first, your punishment won't be as bad as if I find out by myself. You may want to speak up now." She raised her eyebrows.

But then I got an idea. I knew exactly how to get back at Jenna. I knew how to end our fight once and for all: four square.

I smiled. "Really, Mom, everything's fine.
Everything is going to be just fine."

The next day at recess, I marched up to
Jenna. She probably thought I was going to
throw leaves at her head again. But I was so
over that. Before I could say anything, she said,
"Your shoes are ugly!"

I looked at my shoes. They sparkled. I loved
sparkles. "Your jeans are dumb!" I said.

Then we stared at each other. A group of
kids gathered around us.

"Jenna Eastman," I shouted, "I challenge you
to a four-square duel!"

Everyone gasped. For a second, Jenna
looked scared. She should've been. I was really

good at four square. In fact, I was probably the best four-square player in the whole school.

"Um . . . you're challenging me to a what?" she asked.

"A four-square duel," I said.

 "That's dumb," she said. "You can't play four square with two people."

"Can too," I said.

"CANNOT. You have to play TWO square."

"Fine. Whatever. Then I challenge you to a TWO-SQUARE duel."

"Fine. Whatever."

"GOOD!"

"When?" Lacey asked.

"Saturday works for me," I said.

"Deal," Jenna said.

I pumped our hands up and down. "Deal."

I couldn't wait to tell Olive! That night I rushed through supper and took my laptop into my room.

Hi, Olive!

So guess what? I challenged the Liar Tree (Jenna) to a four-square duel! Well, actually, a TWO-SQUARE duel. Isn't that a great idea? I think this is going to solve everything. I just know it.

Love,

Molly

I waited a little bit. Sometimes Olive wrote back right away. Sure enough she did.

Hey, Molly,

Okay. But I thought you were going to tell someone about Jenna being mean. ??? I still think that would be the best thing to do. I just don't want you to get into trouble again.

Love,

Olive

Hmm. That's not what I wanted her to say. I wanted her to say, "Molly, that's a super-great idea!" I wanted her to like my two-square plan. I wanted her to cheer me on. How could I tell Olive I was just as mean as Jenna?

I held my necklace in my hand. Best friends forever. Olive was my best friend. Best friends could tell each other everything, right? Even when they'd done something not-so-great?

Well, Olive, I haven't told you everything . . . I sorta kinda told some lies about Jenna too. I might have said she had head lice (she doesn't) and some other stuff. Sorry I didn't tell you. Do you hate me?

Love,

Molly

Then I sat back and waited to see if I still had a best friend. What if Jenna was right? What if I didn't have any friends? What if I'd lost Olive?

Chapter 6

Queen Awesome's Two-Square Duel

Principal Martinez AND Olive wanted me to talk to Jenna the Liar. I liked both of them a lot — especially Olive of course. But Principal Martinez didn't understand what it's like to be a kid. And Olive didn't understand my school. I couldn't back down now. This two-square duel was serious.

I had three days to get ready. At recess on Wednesday, I saw Jenna sitting alone on the swing. I started to feel bad. Then I shook my head. No, she started this. I was going to end it.

I gathered ten of my classmates, and we played four square every . . . single . . . recess. I was already good at it. I mean, really good. I could hit the corner fast and bounce the ball high. Everyone was talking about me — and in a GOOD way.

I decided I wouldn't tell Olive what was happening. She had a lot on her mind — trying to make new friends and all. I hoped she didn't quit. Olive was sooooo good at gymnastics.

Normally Olive and I wrote every day. But I didn't get an email on Wednesday or Thursday. Strange. I wondered if gymnastics was going okay. I wondered if she was still my friend. I started to feel icky. But I didn't want to send a long email. I didn't want to lie about the duel. So I just sent a quick email.

Olive, I'm rooting for you! Super busy here.
But I hope gymnastics is fun.

Then, to remind her we were best friends, I signed my "superhero" name. Olive and I were both nervous the first day of third grade. So we pretended we were superheroes. My name was Queen Awesome. Olive's was Miss SuperCool. All day I walked around thinking I was Queen Awesome. And you know what? I was! Maybe that would help Olive talk to her teammates. Maybe that would help me win the two-square duel.

I signed off.

Yours forever,

Queen Awesome

On Friday during recess, I got called to the principal's office. I had no idea what I'd done wrong this time.

"Molly, you've been playing A LOT of four square out there," Principal Martinez said.

I nodded. I wanted to say "So?" but that would have gotten me into trouble.

Principal Martinez sat forward and made a triangle with her hands. "I'm afraid some of the other students will feel left out. Their feelings may get hurt."

"Whose feelings?" I asked. First of all I never left anyone out. Second of all only babies tell adults. Although I should have probably told Principal Martinez about Jenna. I could have avoided this two-square mess.

"Does it matter who, Molly? Shouldn't it matter only that someone's feelings are hurt?"

ARE hurt! So someone HAD told on me. Principal Martinez had slipped. "Well, but, how can I say I'm sorry if I don't know who I hurt?" I asked.

"No sorry is necessary," she said. "Just make sure to include everyone in the game from now on. Okay?"

I had a very good idea who was telling on me: someone who looked a lot like a LIAR TREE. But I said, "You got it. I'll make sure to include everybody."

"Good," Principal Martinez said. "I trust you, Molly. I know you have a big heart. Just make sure to listen to it."

Her words smacked into me, hard, like a four-square ball to the head.

Saturday came. It was the day of the duel. I told my mom that I was going to practice soccer at school. "One hour," she said. "Then come straight home."

When I got to school, I saw a big group of kids. Jenna stood in the middle. She looked

scared. Principal Martinez's words came back to me, but I shook my head. I didn't want to hear them again. This was no time for hearts. This was time for two square.

I walked up to the court. Jenna and I stared at each other. I tried to put on my meanest face. Matt, the referee, handed the ball to Jenna.

"The challenged person starts first," he said. "Special rules for the duel. If you mess up, the other person gets a point. For example, if you hit the ball out of bounds, the other person scores. If you let the ball bounce more than once in your square, the other person scores. Got it? First person to score ten points wins."

The crowd got quiet. I cracked my knuckles. A leaf skittered across the squares. Principal Martinez's words still bounced around my

head. I swallowed and looked at the crowd. No one blinked or breathed. I could see sweat on Jenna's forehead.

For a minute I almost called off the whole thing. Everything seemed . . . wrong somehow. I felt like the bully. ME!

But then before I could say anything, Matt yelled, "GO!"

The game began. Jenna served the ball into my square — hard. I returned it, no problem. Jenna was good — real good. Way better than I thought. She hit the ball back high. I smacked it low.

We played for at least five minutes before I made the first mistake. The crowd "oooohed." Jenna smiled. But we were playing to ten

points, so I wasn't worried.
I rolled up my sleeves and
licked my lips.

Jenna served again.
I smacked it back super low.
She didn't stand a chance. Score!

The crowd cheered. I whooped and jumped.
Jenna looked a little scared. I served the
next one and lost the point. Both of us were
sweating now.

Jenna and I hit the ball back and forth. She
would score a point, and then I would score a
point. I stopped worrying about the scared look
on Jenna's face. I wanted to win!

Finally the score was 9–8. I was in the lead.
My serve. Matt handed me the ball. I took a

deep breath. The whole crowd hushed. If I got this point, I'd win the duel. I lifted my arms up really high, like I was going to slam down the ball. And then . . . as fast as I could . . . I squatted down and bounced the ball super, super low.

Jenna was in the middle of a jump because of my amazing fake-out. She missed the ball. Completely. Missed. The ball.

I WON!

The crowd exploded with cheers. Kids chanted my name. "Mol-ly, Mol-ly, Mol-ly!" they shouted. I smiled so big my face hurt. They picked me up and carried me on their shoulders. It was like a parade — a parade for Queen Awesome!

But some of the kids pointed at Jenna and called her a loser. THAT I didn't like. I didn't like that at all. It made my stomach twist into a giant knot. Through the crowd I could see Jenna slump against a tree. I could see her face clearly too. She was crying.

Ugh.

Presenting Miss SuperCool

I wasn't brave enough on Wednesday to write to Molly. I had told her to speak up about Jenna. But I still couldn't say hi to my teammates at the lunch table. I couldn't follow my own advice.

I got a quick email from Molly on Thursday. She signed it "Queen Awesome." That made me smile. I just had to remember I was Miss SuperCool. Except I didn't feel like that. Not at all. I didn't write back.

Finally, Friday after school, I really needed to talk to someone. "Mom!" I yelled when I got home. No answer. I checked the field behind our house.

My parents and I live on a farm. We raise pigs. I have had lots of sows and bulls run at me over the years. And I thought about that as I walked through the pasture. I wasn't scared of a PIG coming at me, but I couldn't say hi to my TEAMMATES. Dumb!

I found my mom in the far corner of the field, fixing a small fence.

"Hey, honey," she said.

"Do you need help?" I asked.

She pointed to part of the fence where the wire was rusted through. "You can start on

that," she said. "Be careful. Don't let the wire poke you."

I nodded. I was glad I had something to do.

After about ten minutes, I said, "Mom, how do you talk to people?"

"What do you mean, honey?" she asked.

"It's just . . ." I began. "I don't think the girls on the team like me. I don't know what to say to them."

"Have you reached out to them?" she asked.

I shook my head. "That's the problem!" I said. "I don't know how to do it. Every time

I try to say hi, I get scared. Or they look super busy. Or sometimes they look mean."

"It can be scary to talk to people you don't know," Mom said. "But you just have to do it. You make new friends that way." She snipped some wire with her clippers. "Sometimes people look mean because they're scared. If you make the first move, maybe you can melt them a little. Just say to yourself, what's the worst that could happen? Well, they could not talk back to you. So what? At least you tried. And you still have Molly as your best friend, right? What have you got to lose?"

I chewed my lip and finished twisting the new wire on the fence. Mom was right. Molly was right. I had to stop worrying and be brave. I had to be Miss SuperCool.

"You're right!" I said, kissing Mom on the cheek and jumping to my feet. "I have to try. What do I have to lose? Thanks, Mom. Time to be Miss SuperCool!"

Mom raised an eyebrow and smiled. She did that a lot at me.

So Saturday I would say hi. Monday I would sit at my teammates' table. I decided not to write Molly about my plans. I wanted to surprise her with some good news — if there was some. If there was BAD news, well . . . I could talk to her about it then.

Saturday morning came, and I got ready to be Miss SuperCool. I was so nervous at practice. My hands were sweating. I got in line for drills and took a deep breath. "I'm SO glad it's Saturday," I said to the girl in front of me.

She turned around, her eyes wide. Before she could say anything, it was her time to go. But I felt good. I had said SOMETHING.

Good Luck!

Then it was Erika's turn for the tumbling drills. Erika is really good at tumbling. Right before she started, I said, "Good luck, Erika!"

She looked at me funny. I swallowed hard. Be Miss SuperCool . . . Be Miss SuperCool . . .

For the rest of the practice, though, I was totally tongue-tied.

I barely slept Sunday night. Monday at lunchtime, I grabbed my tray and walked to my teammates' table. I touched my necklace from Molly for luck. Molly thought I was Miss SuperCool. With her in my corner, I could be a superhero . . . or at least sit down at a lunchroom table.

Erika, Ruth, Haley, and Elsa all looked up and stared at me. My mouth felt like sandpaper. I closed my eyes and said, "Can I sit with you guys?"

It felt like the whole lunchroom stopped to listen. What would my teammates say? My heart was about to jump out of my chest and land in my mashcd potatoes.

Chapter 8

Listen to Your Heart

Molly

I had ten minutes to get home. I was just going to make it. But then my stupid heart got in the way. I couldn't leave Jenna back there crying. She was crying because of me. And I felt terrible.

I texted my mom: 10 XTRA MIN?

My mom wrote back: YES. BUT NO MORE!

When Jenna saw me, she quickly wiped her eyes. "I know you won," she said. "You're better than me. You don't have to rub it in. Everybody loves you."

"Are you crying because you lost?" I asked.

Jenna shook her head and wiped her eyes again. "No," she said. Her voice was real soft.

"Then why?" I played with a loose thread on my shirt. It was easier than looking at Jenna's crying face.

"Because everybody hates me — AGAIN."

Now she had my attention. "What do you mean AGAIN?" I asked.

Jenna shrugged. "This is my tenth school in nine years. I'm always the new kid. I'm always having to make new friends. Just when I start to fit in, I have to move. This time my family is staying a while. But now everyone hates me."

I felt sad for her — and then kind of mad.
I scratched my head. "But why did you say
those things about me?" I asked. "I never did
anything to you! How do you think you'll make
friends if you're mean?"

Jenna started crying again. My heart poked me, but I told it to stop. I had a really good point here.

"I'm sorry I said those things, Molly," Jenna said. "At the other schools, someone ALWAYS picked on me. Always. They'd start mean stories about me, and pretty soon no one would talk to me. This time I thought I'D be the one to start the mean stories. You're so popular, I thought you would be the one who would pick on me. So I chose you."

Boy, did I have a lot of feelings inside me when she said that! I tried to sort them out, one at a time.

"I don't think I'm popular," I began. "But I do talk to everyone at school. Ask around! I am not a shy person."

Jenna smiled a little bit, so I kept talking. "I am not a mean person," I said. I looked away and took a deep breath. "Normally, that is. I'm sorry I made things up about you too, Jenna. I didn't know what to do when you started saying those things. I was confused! But it still wasn't right."

"Thanks," Jenna said.

I took another deep breath. "I'm sorry you got picked on at the other schools. I bet it was really hard — hard to move so much, hard to hear mean stories, hard to make friends . . ."

One thing Olive has taught me as a friend: Always put yourself in the other person's shoes. It seemed like Jenna had been wearing some pretty lousy shoes lately.

I put my hand out to her. She grabbed it and smiled. I pulled her up. "I really am sorry, Molly," she said. "You beat me good!"

I smiled big. "I practiced hard!"

"I know. I saw you!"

Then I remembered my conversation with Principal Martinez. "Did it hurt your feelings that I didn't invite you to play?" I asked.

Jenna shrugged. "Kind of. But I didn't expect you to."

"So why did you tell Principal Martinez on me?" I blurted. "I mean, that's okay. It's okay to tell adults things."

Jenna looked confused. "I didn't say anything. I swear! THIS I'm not lying about."

I looked at her hard, but then we both started laughing. "Hey," I said, "if you help me find out whose feelings I hurt, I'll teach you some killer four-square moves. Deal?"

"Deal," Jenna said, pumping our hands up and down.

That was a much better deal than the last deal we had made. I had to agree with Olive and Principal Martinez: Talking about things does help after all.

When I got home, I sat down and wrote a long letter to Olive. I even drew her a picture. I had a lot to talk about. She'd get it Tuesday.

be happy

Dear Olive,

I have so much to tell you. But first of all — you were right. I should have talked to Jenna or told an adult what was happening. I acted dumb. I'm sorry.

Today was our two-square duel. It was a hard game, but I won! NORMALLY that would've made me happy. But then I saw Jenna crying.

I talked to her, and guess what? She was being mean because people at her other schools were mean to her. She wanted to make sure it didn't happen again. So she bullied first. Except it backfired.

Only it didn't! After we talked, we made a deal. A good deal. I'll tell you about it later. One thing I learned: I like making people feel good, not bad.

ANYWAY, I hope practice is going okay. Write soon!

Your best friend always,

Molly

Chapter 9

Nothing to Lose

Olive

At first I thought maybe I hadn't said the words out loud. So I asked again. "Can I sit with you guys?"

No one said anything. At all. I could feel my cheeks turning tomato red. I got ready to turn around and run. But then Erika said, "Yes! We'd love it if you sat with us!"

So I sat down.

For a minute or so, no one said anything.

I was afraid I'd made a mistake again. Ruth cleared her throat. "We thought about asking you to sit with us," she said, "but it kind of seemed like . . ."

All the girls looked at each other.

"It seemed like what?" I asked.

"Well, like you didn't like us," Erika said.

I almost choked. I didn't like THEM? That was crazy! I started laughing. "I didn't think YOU liked ME!"

Elsa giggled. "Really?" she said.

"Really!" I said.

"That's hilarious!"

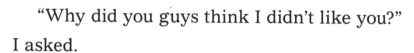

"Why did you guys think I didn't like you?" I asked.

Haley shrugged. "Every time you came near us, you ran away," she said. "And then you didn't say one thing during practice."

Erika smiled. "Except on Saturday. Although I thought at first you were making fun of me."

I almost choked again. I shook my head. "Erika, I would never do that," I said. "It would be mean to do it to anyone. But to a teammate would be the worst." Then I looked at Haley. "I kept trying to get up the courage to say hi to you. Every time I tried, I chickened out. I had no idea it looked like I was running away!" I giggled again. "I mean, I guess I was. But not for the reason it seemed like."

I came clean about everything. Like Mom said, what did I have to lose?

"I was really scared to join the team," I continued. "You guys are much better than me. That first practice . . . I thought you were upset because I was so bad. I know you all have been together for a long time. It just seemed like I should quit."

"No way!" Elsa said.

I nodded. "It's true."

Elsa shook her head. "First of all, you weren't bad to begin with. Second, you've gotten even better — in just a week!"

I smiled HUGE. I was proud of the work I'd done. And they had noticed my effort.

Erika put her hand on my shoulder and squeezed. "We were all the new girl once," she said. "We get it. But you're not new anymore. You can sit here as long as you want."

I had no idea lunch would go so well. It kind of felt like a movie. I was so happy at supper, I couldn't stop humming. I told my parents all about the day — especially the part where we all thought different things.

That got me thinking about Molly. She hadn't written to me all weekend. But to be fair, neither had I. I wondered if we were misunderstanding things. So I wrote her a long email explaining everything.

Hi, Molly,

I'm so sorry I didn't write back to you sooner.
But I wanted to wait until I had some news to share.
And I do have some! I was brave. I finally talked to
my teammates. And guess what? They let me sit with
them at their table. In fact they WANTED me to sit
with them this whole time. We were all too scared to
make the first move!

That made me think about you and Jenna. Is she
scared of something? I really think that's it now. You
REALLY should talk to her. It isn't easy, trust me. But
hey, you're Queen Awesome! Getting things out in
the open feels SO GOOD.

I don't want to go this long again without talking,
okay? No matter what! Even if we feel weird about
something. Because that's what best friends are for!

I hope everything is okay with you. Please write when you can.

Your best friend always,

Miss SuperCool

Everyone Is Welcome

On Monday Jenna and I met at recess. She was all smiles. So was I! I was soooo glad we weren't fighting anymore. We came up with a plan to try to figure out whose feelings I'd hurt. But first things first — I had to set the record straight about Jenna.

I stood on the slide and cupped my hands around my mouth. "Hey, everyone! I want you to know something. Jenna is really cool. Those things I said about her before —" I had a hard time saying this part, but I had to. "Well, they weren't true."

Next Jenna cupped her hands around her mouth and yelled, "Same with what I said about Molly!"

Then she threw her arm around me, and I threw my arm around her. I heard Lacey say, "Oh, brother." But I didn't care. It was a pretty cool moment.

When we got down from the slide, we started Phase One of our plan. Jenna went to get the four-square ball. I walked around the playground and started yelling.

"Hey, ANYONE who wants to play four square, let's go," I said. "Over here! Game's starting!" Lots of kids started coming our

way. Just to be sure, I yelled extra loud, "EVERYONE IS WELCOME!"

"Yeah, we got it," Lacey said. "Geez, you yelled right in my ear."

I just smiled.

We played an awesome four-square game. It didn't seem like anyone had been left out. Later in class Jenna passed me a note: "I know who it is!" I was dying of curiosity. But before I could send back a note, Ms. Harter walked past my desk.

Finally, during free paint hour, Jenna stood by me and my easel. She looked at me and tipped her head toward the corner. There stood a girl I didn't even know was in our class. How did that happen?

"Who is that?" I whispered.

"Her name is Kasey," Jenna whispered back. "Ms. Harter introduced her to us after recess last week. Where were you?"

I thought back. I must have been in Principal Martinez's office. But if Kasey was new, how could I have left her out?

My thoughts ping-ponged all over the place. Then I figured it out. Principal Martinez probably just wanted to make sure I didn't leave Kasey out at all. NO ONE had actually SAID their feelings were hurt. Principal Martinez just didn't want me to leave out any new people.

"Jenna," I said, "new plan." I whispered it to her. She giggled, and then we high-fived.

That hour Jenna and I worked on a painting together. An extra-special painting. Ms. Harter came over to see what we were doing. She liked it! Normally we were supposed to work alone. But she gave us the thumbs-up for this project. Once we were done, we both signed our names in the corner.

"I should have done this for you when you were new," I told Jenna.

And that's when I got a great idea. "We should be the school welcoming club!" I said. "We'll make it our job to make sure new people feel good here."

"That's a great idea, Molly!" Jenna said.

With big smiles we walked over to Kasey.

"Hi, Kasey!" Jenna said. "Molly and I made you something."

We handed Kasey our "Welcome" sign. It had rainbows, the playground, the sun, and Ms. Harter on it. "Glad you're here," I said.

Kasey's eyes got all shiny. "Hey, thanks," she said. "Do you guys play four square?"

Jenna and I laughed. I held out my hand for Kasey to high-five it. "See you at recess," I said.

~ ❀ ~

That night, I got an email from Olive. It was the best email ever. Tomorrow she would get my letter. In the meantime I needed to think of another prank to play on my brother.

But wait! I sat up straight in bed. Was teasing your little brother being mean? I didn't want to be mean. I liked how it felt to make people happy. It felt awesome. And, after all, I was QUEEN Awesome.

Maybe I could teach Damien a few things about four square. I smiled at the thought. I'd email Olive tomorrow and see what she thought. We always came up with the best ideas together.

About the Author

Megan Atwood lives and works in Minneapolis, Minnesota. She has written more than 35 children's books and teaches creative writing at Hamline University. When she is not writing books or teaching, she is inflicting love and affection on her cats and dreaming up more characters to keep her company. She also is trying to find more time to write personal letters to her loved ones, much like Molly and Olive.

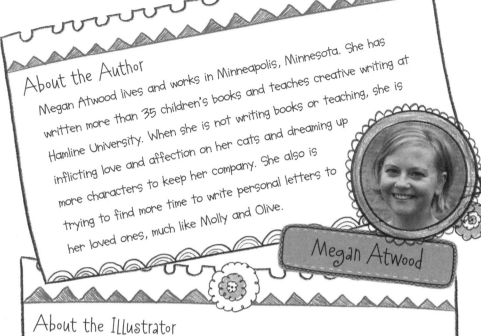

Megan Atwood

About the Illustrator

Lucy Fleming lives and works in a small town in England with an animator and a black cat. She has been an avid doodler and bookworm since early childhood, drawing every day, bringing characters and stories to life. She never dreamed that illustrating would be her job! When not at her desk, Lucy loves to be outdoors in the sunshine with a cup of hot tea — doodling, of course.

Lucy Fleming

Talk It Out

1. Why does Jenna make up the rumor about Molly?

2. What steps does Olive take to make friends on her gymnastics team?

3. What if Molly had asked Jenna right away why she was being mean? Explain how this story would have been different.

Write It Out

1. Write a letter to your best friend. Include all the things that make him or her special.

2. Make a list of ways you can be nice to new students in your class.

3. Describe your favorite recess activity. What do you like about it?

A Letter for You!

Dear friend,

　　Do you know what my favorite place in the whole world is? I'll tell you. It's the Museum of Modern Art (MOMA) here in New York City.

　　MOMA has some really cool stuff. There's this neat event that my mom takes me to called "A Closer Look for Kids." It's great. First the museum people explain some of the art to you. Then you get to do stuff, like paint your own pictures. (My art doesn't look as awesome as Olive's, but I try.) Check out this fun website: www.moma.org/interactives/destination/

　　Anyway, thanks for reading!

Yours truly,

Molly